Shadow Train

ALSO BY JOHN ASHBERY

Poetry

SOME TREES

THE TENNIS COURT OATH

RIVERS AND MOUNTAINS

THE DOUBLE DREAM OF SPRING

THREE POEMS

THE VERMONT NOTEBOOK

SELF-PORTRAIT IN A CONVEX MIRROR

HOUSEBOAT DAYS

AS WE KNOW

Fiction (with James Schuyler)

A NEST OF NINNIES

Plays

THREE PLAYS

Shadow Train

poems by

John Ashbery

THE VIKING PRESS   NEW YORK

First published in 1981 by The Viking Press
625 Madison Avenue, New York, N.Y. 10022
Published simultaneously in Canada by
Penguin Books Canada Limited

LIBRARY OF CONGRESS CATALOGING IN PUBLICATION DATA
Ashbery, John.
Shadow train.
I. Title.
PS3501.S475S5   1981b   811'.54   80-27030
ISBN 0-670-63786-6   AACR1

Grateful acknowledgment is made to the following publications in which
some of these poems originally appeared: *Issues* (Brown University),
"Catalpas"; *New York Review of Books,* "Qualm" and "Caesura"; *The
New Yorker,* "The Pursuit of Happiness"; *Times Literary Supplement,*
"Paradoxes and Oxymorons," "Or in My Throat," and "A Pact with
Sullen Death"; *Yale Review,* "Tide Music" and "Unusual Precau-
tions"; *Zero,* "Night Life" and "But Not That One."

Printed in the United States of America
Set in CRT Caslon

For Richard and Alma Thomas

Contents

Shadow Train

The Pursuit of Happiness

It came about that there was no way of passing
Between the twin partitions that presented
A unified façade, that of a suburban shopping mall
In April. One turned, as one does, to other interests

Such as the tides in the Bay of Fundy. Meanwhile there was one
Who all unseen came creeping at this scale of visions
Like the gigantic specter of a cat towering over tiny mice
About to adjourn the town meeting due to the shadow,

An incisive shadow, too perfect in its outrageous
Regularity to be called to stand trial again,
That every blistered tongue welcomed as the first
Drops scattered by the west wind, and yet, knowing

That it would always ever afterwards be this way
Caused the eyes to faint, the ears to ignore warnings.
We knew how to get by on what comes along, but the idea
Warning, waiting there like a forest, not emptied, beckons.

Punishing the Myth

At first it came easily, with the knowledge of the shadow line
Picking its way through various landscapes before coming
To stand far from you, to bless you incidentally
In sorting out what was best for it, and most suitable,

Like snow having second thoughts and coming back
To be wary about this, to embellish that, as though life were a party
At which work got done. So we wiggled in our separate positions
And stayed in them for a time. After something has passed

You begin to see yourself as you would look to yourself on a stage,
Appearing to someone. But to whom? Ah, that's just it,
To have the manners, and the look that comes from having a secret
Isn't enough. But that "not enough" isn't to be worn like a livery,

To be briefly noticed, yet among whom should it be seen? I haven't
Thought about these things in years; that's my luck.
In time even the rocks will grow. And if you have curled and dandled
Your innocence once too often, what attitude isn't then really yours?

Paradoxes and Oxymorons

This poem is concerned with language on a very plain level.
Look at it talking to you. You look out a window
Or pretend to fidget. You have it but you don't have it.
You miss it, it misses you. You miss each other.

The poem is sad because it wants to be yours, and cannot.
What's a plain level? It is that and other things,
Bringing a system of them into play. Play?
Well, actually, yes, but I consider play to be

A deeper outside thing, a dreamed role-pattern,
As in the division of grace these long August days
Without proof. Open-ended. And before you know
It gets lost in the steam and chatter of typewriters.

It has been played once more. I think you exist only
To tease me into doing it, on your level, and then you aren't there
Or have adopted a different attitude. And the poem
Has set me softly down beside you. The poem is you.

Another Chain Letter

He had had it told to him on the sward
Where the fat men bowl, and told so that no one—
He least of all—might be sure in the days to come
Of the *exact* terms. Then, each turned back

To his business, as is customary on such occasions.
Months and months went by. The green squirearchy
Of the dandelions was falling through the hoop again
And no one, it seemed, had had the presence of mind

To initiate proceedings or stop the wheel
From the number it was backing away from as it stopped:
It was performing prettily; the puncture stayed unseen;
The wilderness seemed to like the eclogue about it

You wrote and performed, but really no one now
Saw any good in the cause, or any guilt. It was a conspiracy
Of right-handed notions. Which is how we all
Became partners in the pastoral doffing, the night we now knew.

The Ivory Tower

Another season, proposing a name and a distant resolution.
And, like the wind, all attention. Those thirsting ears,
Climbers on what rickety heights, have swept you
All alone into their confession, for it is as alone

Each of us stands and surveys this empty cell of time. Well,
What is there to do? And so a mysterious creeping motion
Quickens its demonic profile, bringing tears, to these eyes at least,
Tears of excitement. When was the last time you *knew* that?

Yet in the textbooks thereof you keep getting mired
In a backward innocence, although that too is something
That must be owned, together with the rest.
There is always some impurity. Help it along! Make room for it!

So that in the annals of this year be nothing but what is sobering:
A porch built on pilings, far out over the sand. Then it doesn't
Matter that the deaths come in the wrong order. All has been so easily
Written about. And you find the right order after all: play, the streets,
    shopping, time flying.

Every Evening When the Sun Goes Down

The helmeted head is tilted up at you again
Through a question. Booze and pills?
Probably it has no cachet or real status
Beyond the spokes of the web of good intentions

That radiate a certain distance out from the crater, that is the smile,
That began it? Do you see yourself
Covered by this uniform of half regrets and
Inadmissible satisfactions, dazzling as the shower

Sucked back up into the peacock's-feather eye in the sky
As though through a straw, to connect up with your brain,
The thing given you tonight to wrestle with like an angel
Until dawn? The snuffer says it better. The cone

Squelches the wick, the insulted smoke jerks ceilingward
In the long time since we have been afraid, while the host
Is looking for ice cubes and a glass, is gone
Into the similarity of firmaments. "One last question."

The Freedom of the House

A few more might have survived the fall
To read the afternoon away, navigating
In sullen peace, a finger at the lips,
From the beginning of one surf point to the end,

And again, and may have wondered why being alone
Is the condition of happiness, the substance
Of the golden hints, articulation in the hall outside,
And the condition as well of using that knowledge

To pleasure, always in confinement? Otherwise it fades
Like the rejoicing at the beginning of an opera, since we know
The seriousness of what lies ahead: that we can split open
The ripe exchanges, kisses, sighs, only in unholy

Solitude, and sample them here. It means that a disguised fate
Is weaving a net of heat lightning on the horizon, and that this
Will be neither bad nor good when experienced. Meanwhile
The night has been pushed back again, but cannot say where it has been.

A Pact with Sullen Death

Clearly the song will have to wait
Until the time when everything is serious.
Martyrs of fixed eye, with a special sigh,
Set down their goads. The skies have endured

Too long to be blasted into perdition this way,
And they fall, awash with blood and flowers.
In the dream next door they are still changing,
And the wakening changes too, into life.

"Is this life?" Yes, the last minute was too—
And the joy of informing takes over
Like the crackle of artillery fire in the outer suburbs
And I was going to wish that you too were the "I"

In the novel told in the first person that
This breathy waiting is, that we could crash through
The sobbing underbrush to the laughter that is under the ground,
Since anyone can wait. We have only to begin on time.

White-Collar Crime

Now that you've done it, say OK, that's it for a while.
His fault wasn't great; it was over-eagerness; it didn't deserve
The death penalty, but it's different when it happens
In your neighborhood, on your doorstep; the dropping light spoilt nicely his

Name tags and leggings; all those things that belonged to him,
As it were, were thrown out overnight, onto the street.
So much for fashion. The moon decrees
That it be with us awhile to enhance the atmosphere

But in the long run serious concerns prevail, such as
What time is it and what are you going to do about that?
Gaily inventing brand names, place-names, you were surrounded
By such abundance, yet it seems only fair to start taking in

The washing now. *There was a boy.* Yet by the time the program
Is over, it turns out there was enough time and more than enough things
For everybody to latch on to, and that in essence it's there, the
Young people and their sweet names falling, almost too many of these.

At the Inn

It was me here. Though. And whether this
Be rebus or me now, the way the grass is planted—
Red stretching far out to the horizon—
Surely prevails now. I shall return in the dark and be seen,

Be led to my own room by well-intentioned hands,
Placed in a box with a lid whose underside is dark
So as to grow, and shall grow
Taller than plumes out on the ocean,

Grazing historically. And shall see
The end of much learning, and other things
Out of control and it ends too soon, before hanging up.
So, laying his cheek against the dresser's wooden one,

He died making up stories, the ones
Not every child wanted to listen to.
And for a while it seemed that the road back
Was a track bombarded by stubble like a snow.

The Absence of a Noble Presence

If it was treason it was so well handled that it
Became unimaginable. No, it was ambrosia
In the alley under the stars and not this undiagnosable
Turning, a shadow in the plant of all things

That makes us aware of certain moments,
That the end is not far off since it will occur
In the present and this is the present.
No it was something not very subtle then and yet again

You've got to remember we don't see that much.
We see a portion of eaves dripping in the pastel book
And are aware that everything doesn't count equally—
There is dreaminess and infection in the sum

And since this too is of our everydays
It matters only to the one you are next to
This time, giving you a ride to the station.
It foretells itself, not the hiccup you both notice.

The Prophet Bird

Then take the quicklime to the little tree.
And ask. So all will remain in place, percolating.
You see the sandlots still foaming with the blood of light
Though the source has been withdrawn.

What stunted fig or quince pierced those
Now empty pairs of parentheses. You shout
With the holy feeling of an oppressor, a scourge,
In order for the details to stick,

Like little blades of grass, stubborn and sick.
It is still too many ideas for a landscape.
In another time the tide would have turned, automobiles and the factory
Gushing in to frame the shining, clever, puzzled faces.

There would be even less to pick over, to glean.
But take this idea with you, please. It's all there,
Wrapped up. In the time it takes for nothing to happen
The places, the chairs and tables, the branches, were yours then.

Qualm

Warren G. Harding invented the word "normalcy,"
And the lesser-known "bloviate," meaning, one imagines,
To spout, to spew aimless verbiage. He never wanted to be president.
The "Ohio Gang" made him. He died in the Palace

Hotel in San Francisco, coming back from Alaska,
As his wife was reading to him, about him,
From *The Saturday Evening Post*. Poor Warren. He wasn't a bad egg,
Just weak. He loved women and Ohio.

This protected summer of high, white clouds, a new golf star
Flashes like confetti across the intoxicating early part
Of summer, almost to the end of August. The crowd is hysterical:
Fickle as always, they follow him to the edge

Of the inferno. But the fall is, deliciously, only his.
They shall communicate this and that and compute
Fixed names like "doorstep in the wind." The agony is permanent
Rather than eternal. He'd have noticed it. Poor Warren.

Breezy Stories

"Not spoiling it for later, yet few are
So febrile, so flourishing, and I extract
Digits from the Carolinas to fill out those days in Maine,
Only now trusting myself, as in the latter period I had not yet learned to do."

And on top of all this one must still learn to judge the quality
Of those moments when it becomes necessary to break the rule,
To relax standards, bring light and chaos
Into the order of the house. A slatternly welcome

Suits some as well, no doubt, but the point is
There are still others whom we know nothing about
And who are growing, it seems, at a rate far in excess
Of the legislated norm, for whom the "psychological consequences"

Of the forest primeval of our inconsistency, nay, our lives
If you prefer, and you can quote me, could be "numbing."
Thus, one always reins in, after too much thoughtfulness, the joke
Prescription. Games were made to seem like that: the raw fruit, bleeding.

Oh, Nothing

The tent stitch is repeated in the blue and red
Letters on the blocks. Love is spelled L-O-V-E
And is echoed farther down by fear. These two are sisters
But the youngest and most beautiful sister

Is called Forward Animation. It all makes sense
If you look at her through the clock. Now,
Such towns and benign legends as were distilled
To produce this moment of silence are dissolved

In the stream of history. Of her it may be said
That what she says, she knows, and it will always come undone
Around her, as you are thinking, and so the choice
Is still and always yours, and yet

You may move on, untouched. The glassy,
Chill surface of the cascade reflected her,
Her opinions and future, de-defining you. To be amused this way
Is to be immortal, as water gushes down the sides of the globe.

Of the Islands

Then the thirty-three-year-old man
Then the young but no longer powerfully young man
Gnashed at the towel's edge   chewed the rag
Brought it home to him right out   sighed with the force of

Palm winds: to do it unto others
Is to leave many undone   and the carvings that are "quite cute"
May end up as yours   dry in your storehouse
And this should be good for you yet

"Not as a gift but as a sign of transition"
The way all things spread and seem to remain under the lolling
Fronds and it is not your way as yet.
Only to be an absentee frees from the want of speculation

Drawing out conversations in the lobby   more than you care
And each gift returns home to the bearer   idly, at suppertime
Odd that he noticed you   diminished in this case, but with any
The true respect conserves   the hoofprint in the dust.

Farm Film

Takeitapart, no one understands how you can just do
This to yourself. Balancing a long pole on your chin
And seeing only the ooze of foliage and blue sunlight
Above. At the same time you have not forgotten

The attendant itch, but, being occupied solely with making
Ends meet, or the end, believe that it will live, raised
In secrecy, into an important yet invisible destiny, unfulfilled.
If the dappled cows and noon plums ever thought of

Answering you, your answer would be like the sun, convinced
It knows best, maybe having forgotten someday. But for this
She looked long for one clothespin in the grass, the rime
And fire of midnight etched each other out, into importance

That is like a screen sometimes. So many
Patterns to choose from, they the colliding of all dispirited
Illustration on our lives, that will rise in its time like
Temperature, and mean us, and then faint away.

Here Everything Is Still Floating

But, it's because the liquor of summer nights
Accumulates in the bottom of the bottle.
Suspenders brought it to its, this, level, not
The tempest in a teapot of a private asylum, laughter on the back steps,

Not mine, in fine; I must concentrate on how disappointing
It all has to be while rejoicing in my singular
Un-wholeness that keeps it an event to me. These, these young guys
Taking a shower with the truth, living off the interest of their

Sublime receptivity to anything, can disentangle the whole
Lining of fabricating living from the instantaneous
Pocket it explodes in, enters the limelight of history from,
To be gilded and regilded, waning as its legend waxes,

Disproportionate and triumphant. Still I enjoy
The long sweetness of the simultaneity, yours and mine, ours and mine,
The mosquitoey summer night light. Now about your poem
Called this poem: it stays and must outshine its welcome.

Joe Leviathan

Just because I wear a voluminous cap
With a wool-covered wooden button at its peak, the cries of children
Are upon me, passing through me. The season at this time
Offers no other spectacle for the curious part-time executioner.

In his house they speak of rope. They skate past the window.
I have seen and know
Bad endings lumped with the good. They are in the future
And therefore cannot be far off.

The bank here is quite steep
And casts its shadow over the river floor.
An exploration, a field trip, might be worth making.
We could have made some nice excursions together.

Then he took a bat and the clams and
Where hope is the door it is stained with the strong stench of brine.
Inside too. The window frames have been removed. I mean
He can pass with me in the meaning and we still not see ourselves.

Some Old Tires

This was mine, and I let it slip through my fingers.
Nevertheless, I do not want, in this airy and pleasant city,
To be held back by valors that were mine
Only for the space of a dream instant, before continuing

To be someone else's. Because there's too much to
Be done that doesn't fit, and the parts that get lost
Are the reasonable ones just because they got lost
And were forced to suffer transfiguration by finding their way home

To a forgotten spot way out in the fields. To have always
Had the wind for a friend is no recommendation. Yet some
Disagree, while still others claim that signs of fatigue
And mended places are, these offshore days, open

And a symbol of what must continue
After the ring is closed on us. The furniture,
Taken out and examined under the starlight, pleads
No contest. And the backs of those who sat there before.

A Prison All the Same

Spoken over a yellow kitchen table (just the ticket
For these recycling-minded times): *You've got to show them who you are.*
Just being a person doesn't work anymore. Many of them drink beer.
A crisis or catastrophe goes off in their lives

Every few hours. They don't get used to it, having no memory.
Nor do they think it's better that way. What happens for them
Is part of them, an appendage. There's no room to step back
To get a perspective. The old one shops and thinks. The fragrant bulbs

In the cellar are no use either. Last week a man was here.
But just try sorting it out when you're on top
Of your destiny, like angels elbowing each other on the head of a pin.
Not until someone falls, or hesitates, does the renewal occur,

And then it's only for a second, like a breath of air
On a hot, muggy afternoon with no air conditioning. I was scared
Then. Now it's over. It can be removed like a sock
And mended, a little. One for the books.

Drunken Americans

I saw the reflection in the mirror
And it doesn't count, or not enough
To make a difference, fabricating itself
Out of the old, average light of a college town,

And afterwards, when the bus trip
Had depleted my pocket of its few pennies
He was seen arguing behind steamed glass,
With an invisible proprietor. What if you can't own

This one either? For it seems that all
Moments are like this: thin, unsatisfactory
As gruel, worn away more each time you return to them.
Until one day you rip the canvas from its frame

And take it home with you. You think the god-given
Assertiveness in you has triumphed
Over the stingy scenario: these objects are real as meat,
As tears. We are all soiled with this desire, at the last moment, the last.

Something Similar

I, the city mouse, have traveled from a long ways away
To be with you with my news. Now you have my passport
With its color photo in it, to be sweet with you
As the times allow. I didn't say that because it's true,

I said it from a dim upstairs porch into the veiled
Shapely masses of this country you are the geography of
So you can put it in your wallet. That's all we can do
For the time being. Elegance has been halted for the duration

And may not be resumed again. The bare hulk tells us
Something, but mostly about what a strain it was to be brought
To such a pass, and then abandoned. So we may never
Again feel fully confident of the stratagem that bore us

And lived on a certain time after that. And it went away
Little by little, as most things do. To profit
By this mainstream is today's chore and adventure. He
Who touches base first at dusk is possessed first, then wins.

Penny Parker's Mistake

That it could not be seen as constituting an endorsement
Any way she looked, up, down, around, around again, always the same
For her, always her now, was in the way it winked back.
For naturally, to be selling these old Indian dinosaur

Eggs and to be in some obscure way in their debt, not
For the modest living they provided, rather in having come to know
Them at all (not everybody need know everybody, and when you
Stop to think of it, this fits each of us tighter than

Any of the others) was the throwback to the earlier
Age each dreamed, a dream with little gold flecks
And reflection of wet avenues in the japanned facing of it.
Now, naturally we caring for the success of the success

Cannot cancel postures from some earlier decade of this century
That come to invade our walking like the spokes of an umbrella
And in some real way undermine the heaven of attitudes our chance was.
To be uncoiling this way, now, is the truer, but slier, stage of inebriation.

Or in My Throat

To the poet as a basement quilt, but perhaps
To some reader a latticework of regrets, through which
You can see the funny street, with the ends of cars and the dust,
The thing we always forget to put in. For him

The two ends were the same except that he was in one
Looking at the other, and all his grief stemmed from that:
There was no way of appreciating anything else, how polite
People were for instance, and the dream, reversed, became

A swift nightmare of starlight on frozen puddles in some
Dread waste. Yet you always hear
How they are coming along. Someone always has a letter
From one of them, asking to be remembered to the boys, and all.

That's why I quit and took up writing poetry instead.
It's clean, it's relaxing, it doesn't squirt juice all over
Something you were certain of a minute ago and now your own face
Is a stranger and no one can tell you it's true. Hey, stupid!

Untilted

How tall the buildings were as I began
To live, and how high the rain that battered them!
Why, coming down them, as I often did at night,
Was a dream even before you reached the first gullies

And gave yourself over to thoughts of your own welfare.
It was the tilt of the wine in the cavalier's tilted glass
That documents so unerringly the faces and the mood in the room.
One slip would not be fatal, but then this is not a win or lose

Situation, so involved with living in the past on the ridge
Of the present, hearing its bells, breathing in its steam. . . .
And the shuttle never falters, but to draw an encouraging conclusion
From this would be considerable, too odd. Why not just

Breathe in with the courage of each day, recognizing yourself as one
Who must with difficulty get down from high places? Forget
The tourists—other people must travel too. It hurts now,
Cradled in the bend of your arm, the pure tear, doesn't it?

At Lotus Lodge

After her cat went away she led a quiet but remarkable
Existence. No tandem ways, but once out of town
The boxcars alternated with scenes of the religious life
In strong, faded colors. There is something in every room

Of the house, and in the powder room one truly inconceivable thing
That doesn't matter and is your name. You arrived late last night.
In between then and now is a circle for sleeping in
And we are right, at such moments, not to worry about the demands of others;

They are like trees planted on a slope, too preoccupied
With the space dividing them to notice this singular tale of the past
And the thousand stories just like it, until one spills over
Into dreams, and they can point to it and say, "That's a dream,"

And go about their business. There is no compelling reason
For this moment to insist, yet it does, and has been with us
Down from the time England and Scotland were separate monarchies. She got
No reply for your question, but that's understandable. All she had to do was lie.

Corky's Car Keys

Despite, or because
Of its rambunctiousness, Kevin and Tracy—only appearances
Matter much—lingered in the not-night, red-painted brick background
Of festivals. And trees, old

Trees, like that one—sweet white dreams
Contain them, "in and out the windows."
Are the sunsets faster, now in old age, now
That you are inundated with them, or with something

To know me better? Yet despite, or because of, that, we have
To live here, so we should fix
This place up. A long time ago, in some earlier revival,
It seemed one of many handsome, felicitous choices—

How quickly the years pass. How could we tell the sound
Of the city at night would grow up too? And in its uncomfortable
Maturity dictate pyramids, process orders? Yet we can regulate
Everything in a little while, if he is truly the steeple.

Night Life

I thought it was you but I couldn't tell.
It's so hard, working with people, you want them all
To like you and be happy, but they get in the way
Of their own predilections, it's like a stone

Blocking the mouth of a cave. And when you say, come on let's
Be individuals reveling in our separateness, yet twined
Together at the top by our hair, like branches, then it's OK
To go down into the garden at night and smoke cigarettes,

Except that nothing cares about the obstacles, the gravity
You had to overcome to reach this admittedly unimpressive
Stage in the chain of delusions leading to your freedom,
Or is that just one more delusion? Yet I like the way

Your hair is cropped, it's important, the husky fragrance
Breaking out of your voice, when I've talked too long
On the phone, addressing the traffic from my balcony
Again, launched far out over the thin ice once it begins to smile.

Written in the Dark

Telling it five, six, seven times a day,
Telling it like a bedtime story no one knows,
Telling it like a fortune, that happened a short time ago,
Like yesterday afternoon, so recently that it seems not to have

Quite happened yet. . . . All these and more were ways
Our love assumed to look like a state religion,
Like political wisdom. It's too bad that the two hands
Clenched between us fail us in their concreteness,

That we need some slogan to transform it all into autumn
Banners streaming, into flutter of bronze oak leaves, a surface
As intense and inquisitive as that of the sea. We stayed home.
We drank table wine, yellow then violet, wormwood color,

Color of the sound of waves sweeping across a flat beach
Farther than ever before, taking greater liberties in the name
Of liberty. But it shouldn't. Don't you see how there can be
Exceptions, even to this, this firmament, graciousness that is home?

Caesura

Job sat in a corner of the dump eating asparagus
With one hand and scratching his unsightly eruptions
With the other. Pshaw, it'd blow over. In the office
They'd like discussing it. His thoughts

Were with the office now: how protected it was,
Though still a place to work. Sit up straight, the
Monitor inside said. It worked for a second
But didn't improve the posture of his days, taken

As a cross section of the times. Correction: of our time.
And it was (it was again): "Have you made your list up?
I have one ambulance three nuns two (black-
And-white list) cops dressed as Keystone Kops lists, a red light

At leafy intersection list." Then it goes blank, pulp-color.
Until at the end where they give out the list
Of awardees. The darkness and light have returned. It was still
The weather of the soul, vandalized, out-at-elbow. A blight. Spared, though.

The Leasing of September

The sleeping map lay green, and we who were never much
To begin with, except for what the attractiveness of youth
Contributed, stood around in the pastures of heaped-up, thickened
White light, convinced that the story was coming to a close,

Otherwise why all these figurines, the Latin freemasonry in the corners?
You stepped into a blue taxi, and as I swear my eyes were in keeping
With the beauty of you as they saw it, so a swallow perpetuated
In dove-gray dusk can be both the end and the exaltation of a new

Beginning, yet forever remain itself, as you
Seem to run alongside me as the car picks up speed. Is it
Your hand then? Will I always then return
To the tier upon tier of cloth layered in the closet

Against what departure? Even a departure from the normal?
So we are not recognized, under the metal. But to him
The love was a solid object, like a partly unpacked trunk,
As it was then, which is different now when remembered.

On the Terrace of Ingots

It was the bitterness of the last time
That only believers and fools take for the next time
Proposing itself as a chore against an expressionist
Backdrop of skylights and other believed finial flourishes, and

You wash your hands, become a duct to drain off
All the suffering of the age you thought you had
Put behind you in defining it, but the sense mounts
Slowly in the words as in a hygrometer—that day

You stood apart from the class in the photograph.
The trees seemed to make a little sense, more precious
Than anything on earth. For the clamor
Was drawing it all away, as in a parade; you saw

How much smaller it all kept getting. And the fathers
Failed. I don't think it would be different today
If we are alone up here. The flares of today
Aren't like suffering either, yet are almost everyone.

Tide Music

Again in the autumn there is a case for it,
The tastelessness that just curls up and sometimes dies
At the edge of certain thoughtful, uneventful sidewalks.
In the afternoon you can hear what you can't see, all around,

The patterns of distress settling into rings
Of warm self-satisfaction and disbelief, as though
The whole surface of the air and the morrow were scored
Over and over with a nail as heavy rains

Pounded the area, until underneath all was revealed as mild,
Transient shining, the way a cloud dissolves
Around the light that is of its own making, hard as it is
To believe, and as though the welcoming host in you had

For some reason left the door to the street open and all
Kinds of amiable boors had taken advantage of it, though the mat
Isn't out. All the sky, each ragged leaf, have been thoroughly gone over
And every inch is accounted for in the tune, the wallpaper of dreams.

Unusual Precautions

"We, we children, why our lives are circumscribed, circumferential;
Close, too close to the center, we are haunted by perimeters
And our lives seem to go in and out, in and out all the time,
As though yours were diagonal, vertical, shallow, chopped off

At the root like the voice of the famous gadfly: 'Oh! Aho!' it
Sits in the middle of the roadway. That's it. Worry and brown desk
Stain it by infusion. There aren't enough tags at the end,
And the grove is blind, blossoming, but we are too porous to hear it.

It's like watching a movie of a nightmare, the many episodes
That defuse the thrust of what comes to us. The girl who juggled Indian clubs
Belongs again to the paper space that backs the black
Curtain, as though there were a reason to have paid for these seats.

Tomorrow you'll be walking in a white park. Our interests
Are too close for us to see. There seems to be no
Necessity for it, yet in walking, we too, around, and all around
We'll come to one, where the street crosses your name, and feet run up it."

Flow Blue

It may sound like a lot of odds and cloud-filled
Ends—at best, a thinking man's charmed fragment, perhaps
A house. And it could be that father and sky—
Moments so far gone into decay, as well as barely

Rating entry into a stonemason's yard—from the very first moment
Need no persuading: we know that the sky sits,
That these are sculptures of singular detail
Separate to a particular society. The black jell-like

Substance pours from the eye into the tower in the field,
Making uneasy acceptance. There were differences when
Only you knew them, and the grass was gray, escaping the houses,
The septic tank and the fields. Lost, I found the small stand

In the wood. It was funny and quiet there. And I know now how
This is not a place where I could stay. The endless ladder being carried
Past our affairs, like strings in a hop-field, decants
A piano-tuning we feed on as it dances us to the edge.

Hard Times

Trust me. The world is run on a shoestring.
They have no time to return the calls in hell
And pay dearly for those wasted minutes. Somewhere
In the future it will filter down through all the proceedings

But by then it will be too late, the festive ambience
Will linger on but it won't matter. More or less
Succinctly they will tell you what we've all known for years:
That the power of this climate is only to conserve itself.

Whatever twists around it is decoration and can never
Be looked at as something isolated, apart. Get it? And
He flashed a mouthful of aluminum teeth there in the darkness
To tell however it gets down, that it does, at last.

Once they made the great trip to California
And came out of it flushed. And now every day
Will have to dispel the notion of being like all the others.
In time, it gets to stand with the wind, but by then the night is closed off.

"Moi, je suis la tulipe . . ."

And you get two of everything. Twin tunics, the blue
And the faded. And are wise for today, allowing as how people,
Dressing up in their way, will repeat your blunder out of kindness
So it won't happen again. Seriously, the magazines speak of you,

Mention you, a lot. I have seen the articles and the ads recently.
Your name is on everyone's lips. Nobody comes to see us, because
You have to forget yourself in order to forget other people,
At which point the game is under way. My personality fades away

As dreams evaporate by day, which stays, with the dream
Materials in solution, cast out in a fiery precipitate
Later with people on their way, on parade in a way, and all kinds
Of things. All men are ambiguous and

They sometimes have hairy chests, in a long line
Of decayed and decaying ancestors. Fine in my time, I
Know that I am still, but that there is a blur around
The hole that hatches me into reason, surprised, somewhat, but sure.

Catalpas

All around us an extraordinary effort is being made.
Something is in the air. The tops of trees are trying
To speak to this. The audience for these events is amazed,
Can't believe them, yet is walking in its sleep,

By twos and threes, on the ramparts in the moonlight.
Understanding must be introduced now, at no matter what cost.
Nature wants us to understand in many ways
That the age of noyades is over, although danger still lurks

In the enormous effrontery that appearances put on things,
And will continue to for some time. But all this comes as no surprise;
You knew the plot before, and expected to arrive in this place
At the appointed time, and now it's almost over, even

As it's erupting in huge blankets of forms and solemn,
Candy-colored ideas that you recognize as your own,
Only they look so strange up there on the stage, like the light
That shines through sleep. And the third day ends.

We Hesitate

The days to come are a watershed.
You have to improve your portrait of God
To make it plain. It is on the list,
You and your bodies are on the line.

The new past now unfurls like a great somber hope
Above the treeline, like a giant's hand
Placed tentatively on the hurrying clouds.
The basins come to be full and complex

But it is not enough. Concern and embarrassment
Grow rank. Once they have come home there is no cursing.
Fires disturb the evening. No one can hear the story.
Or sometimes people just forget

Like a child. It took me months
To get that discipline banned, and what is the use,
To ban that? You remain a sane, yet sophisticated, person:
Rooted in twilight, dreaming, a piece of traffic.

The Desperado

What kind of life is this that we are leading
That so much strong vagary can slip by unnoticed?
Is there a future? It seems that all we'd planned
To find in it is rolling around now, spending itself.

You step aside, and the rock invasion from the fifties
Dissipates in afternoon smoke. And disco
Retreats a little, wiping large brown eyes.
They come along here. Now, all will be gone.

I am the shadowed, widower, the unconsoled.
But if it weren't for me I should also be the schoolmaster
Coaching, pruning young spring thoughts
Surprised to be here, in this air.

But their barely restrained look suits the gray
Importance of what we expect to be confronted with
Any day. Send the odious one a rebuke. Can one deny
Any longer that it is, and going to be?

The Image of the Shark Confronts
the Image of the Little Match Girl

With a stool on your head you
Again find yourself in that narrow alley
That threads the whole center of the city.
"They're not nice people today is not nice"

Is the austere bleat and the helpful hints
On the back are overlooked, just as before.
I know whose agents have set feet on this way,
This time. And the sky is unforgettable.

Take a sip of your mother's drink. It was told
Long ago in the Borodin string quartet how the mists
And certain other parts of antediluvian forests still
Hassle this downtown mysteriously, and sometimes

The voice of reason is heard for a hard, clear moment,
Then falls still, if for no other reason than
That the sheriff's deputies have suddenly coincided
With a collective notion of romance, and the minute has absconded.

Songs Without Words

Yes, we had gone down to the shore
That year and were waiting for the expected to happen
According to a preordained system of its own devising.
Its people were there for decoration,

Like notes arranged on a staff. What you made of them
Depended on your ability to read music and to hear more
In the night behind them. It gave us
A kind of amplitude. And the watchmen were praying

So long before rosy-fingered dawn began to mess around
With the horizon that you wondered, yet
It made a convenient bridge to pass over, from starlight
To the daylit kingdom. I don't think it would have been any different

If the ships hadn't been there, poised, flexing their muscles,
Ready to take us where they pleased and that country had been
Rehabilitated and the sirens, la la, stopped singing
And canceled our melting protection from the sun.

Indelible, Inedible

Work had been proceeding at a snail's pace
Along the river, and now that the spring torrents had begun
We kept our distance from the mitered flashing,
The easy spoke-movement of the hopeless expanse

Caught, way out in the distance, with a thread of meaning
Which was fear. Some things are always left undecided
And regroup, to reappear next year in a new light,
The light of change. And the moods are similar

Too the second time around, only more easy of access.
You can talk to each other, sheltered now,
As though just inside the flap of a big circus tent
And leave whenever you want to. Nothing could be easier.

That was then. And its enduring lasted through many
Transformations, before it came to seem as though it could not be done.
Cats were curious about it. They followed it
Down into the glen where it was last seen.

School of Velocity

Urban propinquities extrude a wood-pegged
(In the imperialist taste) balcony just above
The heads of penitents as their parade
Turns the corner and is seen no more. Coleridge-Taylor

Or a hare-shaped person is somehow involved;
His aquarelle takes on meaning, and a cloud
Is suddenly torn asunder so that the green heartbreak
Of the eternally hysterical sun hoses down the gutters

And tender walkways where we first became aware
Of a confession and trees that were on one side only.
Probably they wear out the light with too much fussing
Otherwise and yet the landscape looks strangely neglected.

An orphan. We are overheard,
As usual. We're sorry, I say. The houses, the puddles,
Even the cars are pegs. One who noticed the street flooded
Calls out in time. Tomorrow the procession returns, and what then?

Frontispiece

Expecting rain, the profile of a day
Wears its soul like a hat, prow up
Against the deeply incised clouds and regions
Of abrupt skidding from cold to cold, riddles

Of climate it cannot understand.
Sometimes toward the end
A look of longing broke, taut, from those eyes
Meeting yours in final understanding, late,

And often, too, the beginnings went unnoticed
As though the story could advance its pawns
More discreetly thus, overstepping
The confines of ordinary health and reason

To introduce in another way
Its fact into the picture. It registered,
It must be there. And so we turn the page over
To think of starting. This is all there is.

Everyman's Library

> . . . the sparrow hath found an house,
> and the swallow a nest for herself . . .
>
> PSALM 84

In the outlying districts where we know something
The sparrows don't, and each house
Is noticeably a little nicer than the rest, the "package"
Is ready to be performed now. It comes

As a sheaf of papyruslike, idle imaginings
And identifyings, and stays put like that.
It's beginning to get darker. You send someone
Down the flight of stairs to ask after

The true course of events and the answer always
Comes back evasive yet polite: you have only to step down . . .
Oops, the light went out. That is the paper-thin
But very firm dimension of ordinary education. And when a thief

Is out there, in the dark somewhere, it also applies.
There is no freedom, and no freedom from freedom.
The only possible act is to pick up the book, caress it
And open it in my face. You knew that.

Shadow Train

Violence, how smoothly it came
And smoothly took you with it
To wanting what you nonetheless did not want.
It's all over if we don't see the truth inside that meaning.

To want is to be better than before. To desire what is
Forbidden is permitted. But to desire it
And not want it is to chew its name like a rag.
To that end the banana shakes on its stem,

But the strawberry is liquid and cool, a rounded
Note in the descending scale, a photograph
Of someone smiling at a funeral. The great plumes
Of the dynastic fly-whisk lurch daily

Above our heads, as far up as clouds. Who can say
What it means, or whether it protects? Yet it is clear
That history merely stretches today into one's private guignol.
The violence dreams. You are half-asleep at your instrument table.

But Not That One

The works, the days, uh,
And weariness of the days
Gradually getting a little longer,
Turning out to be a smile, everything

Like that. And it does make a difference,
Oh it does. Because the smile is a different not us,
Ready to rescind, cancel,
Rip out the stitches of the sky,

Then it warmed up. O a lot
Blooms, gets squashed on the tongue:
Where are you going? Who do you think you are?
Crushed leaves, berries, the stars

Continually falling, streaking the sky:
Can it be the context? No, it is old and
Sometimes the agog spectator wrenches a cry
From its own house. He thought he heard.

The Vegetarians

In front of you, long tables leading down to the sun,
A great gesture building. You accept it so as to play with it
And translate when its attention is deflated for the one second
Of eternity. Extreme patience and persistence are required,

Yet everybody succeeds at this before being handed
The surprise box lunch of the rest of his life. But what is
Truly startling is that it all happens modestly in the vein of
True living, and then that too is translated into something

Floating up from it, signals that life flashed, weak but essential
For uncorking the tone, and now lost, recently but forever.
In Zurich everything was pure and purposeful, like the red cars
Swung around the lake on wires, against the sky, then back down

Through the weather. Which resembles what you want to do
No more than black tree trunks do, though you thought of it.
Therefore our legends always come around to seeming legendary,
A path decorated with our comings and goings. Or so I've been told.